The
Big Blue Spot

The Big Blue Spot

by
Peter Holwitz

Philomel Books New York

This is the spot.
The BIG BLUE SPOT.
It doesn't do much.
Spots never do.
It spends each day
just being blue.

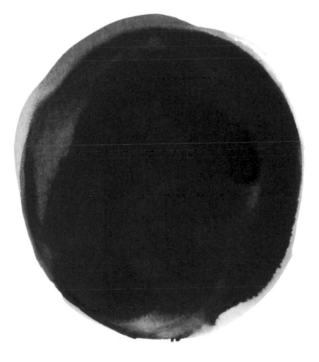

It's here when it's cold.
It's here when it's hot.
It's here when YOU'RE here.
It's here when you're not.
It is what it is.
A BIG BLUE SPOT.
It has what it needs,
and that's not a lot.

Until one day.
This day, in fact.
That big blue spot thought of
something it lacked.
It opens its eyes

right out of the blue.

Two friendly eyes look up at you.

"Excuse me,"
it says. Its mouth opens white.
"Would you tip this book
just a bit to the right?"
So you do. Well, why not?
When was the last time
you spoke with a spot?

Then it got weird.
That spot disappeared.

It dripped off the page, right over the text.
Right off the page and onto the next.

EXTENSION

You try to catch up,

but that spot is too quick.

The faster you turn,

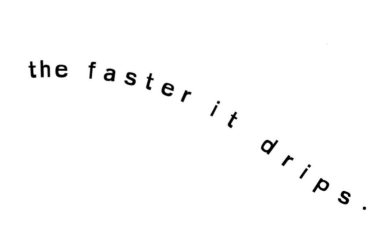

the f a s t e r i t d r i p s .

So you yell to the spot,

"**Hey,** wait a minute.

This is my book,
and you belong in it!"

Then it stops where it's at.
Big, blue and flat.
It looks up at you and says,

"I know that. But I've lived in this book
since I've been a spot,
and up until now, I've liked it a lot.

Am I the only spot in this book?
If I am, then I am,
but I'd still like to look."

"I understand," you say to the spot.
"I have friends,
and I love them a lot.

If there's another spot in this book,
we'll find it for sure.
I'll help you look."

So you tip the book just a bit to the right,

and that big blue spot drips right out of sight.

Curious now, you follow along.

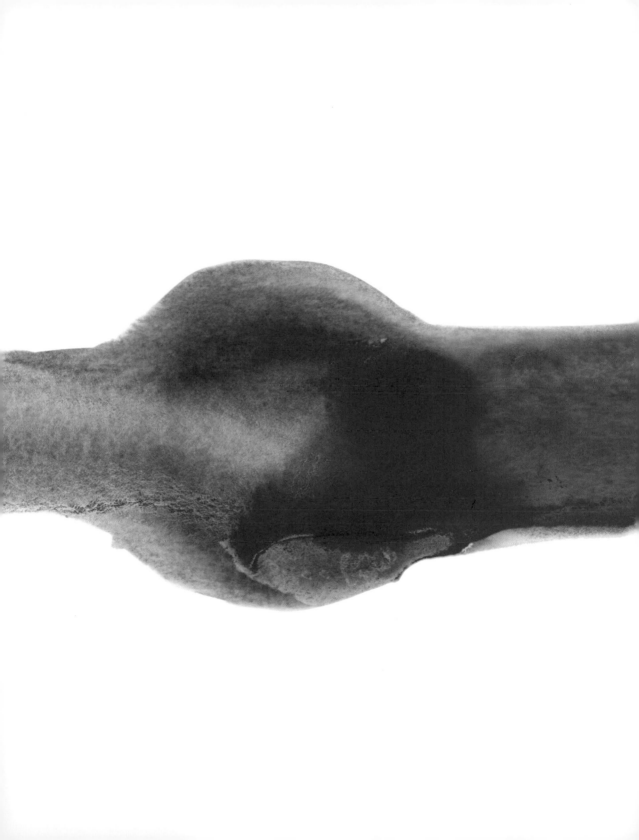

It drips.

And it drips.

And then, before long . . .

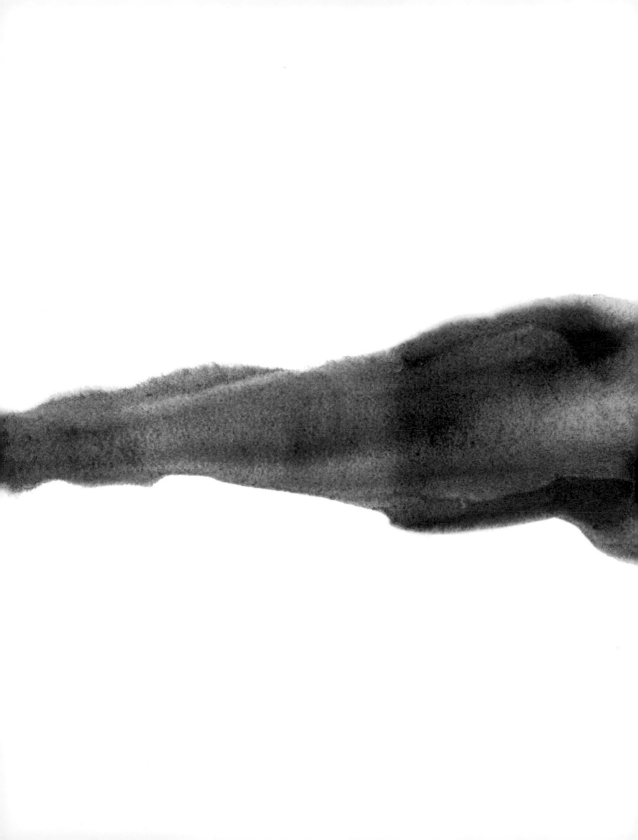

On the very next page,
just a few from the end,
that big blue spot finds a beautiful friend.

"How do you do?"
asks the big blue spot.

"I do well," she replies,
"but I don't do a lot."
Then that big yellow spot looks up at you.
She smiles wide, and you know what to do.
You hold up the book, and close it a little . . .

And those two big spots
drip right toward the middle.

What a mess they make,
the biggest you've seen.
Yellow and blue, and a little green.

"Thank you," they say.
"It's nice to have a friend.

If you need us, we're here.
In this book, at **THE END**."

To Mom & Dad